RUBIA

and the

THREE OSOS

This **LIBRO** belongs to:

RUBIA
and the
THREE OSOS

written by
Susan Middleton Elya

illustrated by
Melissa Sweet

SCHOLASTIC INC.

There once were three OSOS
who lived by themselves.

They stored their three platos
for soup on the shelves.

But one night at supper
—la sopa prepared,

the soup platos ladled,
the chairs derriere'd—

Mamá said, "Let's go for a walk before dinner.
It's part of my South Woods Plan, so I'll be thinner."

Papá rolled his eyes, but he still nodded, "Sí."

Bebé pushed his cubby car after them. Whee!
They headed away, but the door wasn't locked.
Then who should come over, so daintily frocked?

Little Miss **Rubia**, curls made of oro.
"¿A tiny casita, for me? ¡La adoro!"

She opened la puerta and saw the fine food.
"¡Sopa!" she said. "I am *so* in the mood!"
The big bowl was steaming—caliente, too hot,
and the middle one—frío. "What else have they got?
¡Eso!" She spotted the tiniest bowl.

"¡PERFECTO!"
she blurted, and then drank it whole.

She noticed three sillas, where she could sit down:
the big one—too dura. It made the girl frown.
The middle one—suave, but it wouldn't do.

The tiny one—great, till she broke it in two.

The soup made her sleepy. She headed upstairs,
and found las tres camas for all of the bears.
La grande was hard, the middle one—soft.

But there was a little bed up in the loft.
The small one was **buena**, so that's where she lay.

Then here came Papá, Mamá, and Bebé.
They opened the door and noticed la mesa
where one bowl sat empty, Bebé's sad sorpresa.

"¡MI SOPA!" he yelled. He started to cry.
"They didn't just eat it, they licked the bowl dry."

¡OO₀OHHHHH!

Mamá saw his silla.

"Oh, what have they done?"

¡GRRRrrr!

Papá growled in anger.
"The Perp better run!"

Just then little **Rubia** sat up in the bed.
"This home isn't mine. It's for those guys instead!"

She dashed for the window and jumped to a tree.
Soon she was chased by the angry bears three.

They ran right behind her, but she had good speed.
THE GIRL GOT AWAY!

Then she did a good deed.

She came back with SOPA, along with some glue.
"Lo siento," she said, "especially to you."

She served Bebé soup and helped patch his silla,
then gave him a ride in his cub carretilla.

"Stay," said Mamá as she kneaded some masa.

"Sí," said Papá. "Our house es tu casa."

Rubia felt love from the family Oso, and having their friendship was great—

¡FABULOSO!

·GLOSSARY·

Bebé (beh BEH) Baby

bienvenido (byehn veh NEE doe) welcome

buena (BWEH nah) good

caliente (kah LYEHN teh) hot

(la) carretilla (kah rreh TEE yah) (the) cubby car

(la) casa (KAH sah) (the) house

(la) casita (kah SEE tah) (the) cottage

dura (DOO rah) hard

es tu casa (EHS TOO KAH sah) is your house

eso (EH soe) that one

fabuloso (fah boo LOE soe) fabulous

frío (FREE oe) cold

la (LAH) the*

la adoro (lah ah DOE roe) I adore it

la grande (LAH GRAHN deh) the big one

las tres camas (LAHS TREHS KAH mahs) the three beds

(el) libro (LEE broe) (the) book

lo siento (LOE SYEHN toe) I'm sorry

* el, los, and las can also mean "the"

los osos (LOCE OE soce) the bears

Mamá (mah MAH) Mom

(la) masa (MAH sah) (the) dough

(la) mesa (MEH sah) (the) table

mi sopa (MEE SOE pah) my soup

oro (OE roe) gold

(el) oso (OE soe) (the) bear

Papá (pah PAH) Dad

Perfecto (pehr FEHK toe) Perfect

(los) platos (PLAH toce) (the) plates, bowls

(la) puerta (PWEHR tah) (the) door

Rubia (RROO byah) Goldie, a blonde

sí (SEE) yes

(las) sillas (SEE yahs) (the) chairs

(la) sopa (SOE pah) (the) soup

(la) sorpresa (sohr PREH sah) (the) surprise

suave (SWAH veh) soft

To Elaine in Georgia, far away in miles,
but still a close friend — S. M. E.

To my amigas Alison and Jone — M. S.

ISBN 978-0-545-55092-5

Text copyright © 2010 by Susan Middleton Elya.
Illustrations copyright © 2010 by Melissa Sweet.
All rights reserved. Published by Scholastic Inc.,
557 Broadway, New York, NY 10012,
by arrangement with Hyperion Books for Children,
an imprint of Disney Book Group, LLC.
SCHOLASTIC and associated logos are trademarks
and/or registered trademarks of Scholastic Inc.

12 11 10 9 8 7 6 5 4 3 2 1   13 14 15 16 17 18/0

Printed in the U.S.A.   08

This edition first printing, January 2013

The art was created in watercolor and mixed media.
Designed by Scott Piehl